This book belongs to

Remy

Copyright © 2019

make believe ideas ltd

The Wilderness, Berkhamsted, Hertfordshire, HP4 2AZ, UK.

www.makebelieveideas.com

Written by Rosie Greening.
Illustrated by Lara Ede.

Meghan Sparkle
and the ROYAL BABY

Lara Ede · Rosie Greening

make
believe
ideas

Once, in **Coral Kingdom**, an announcement came to say that a brand-new **royal baby** had been born that very day!

The King &
Queen have
a new baby
called Bubble!

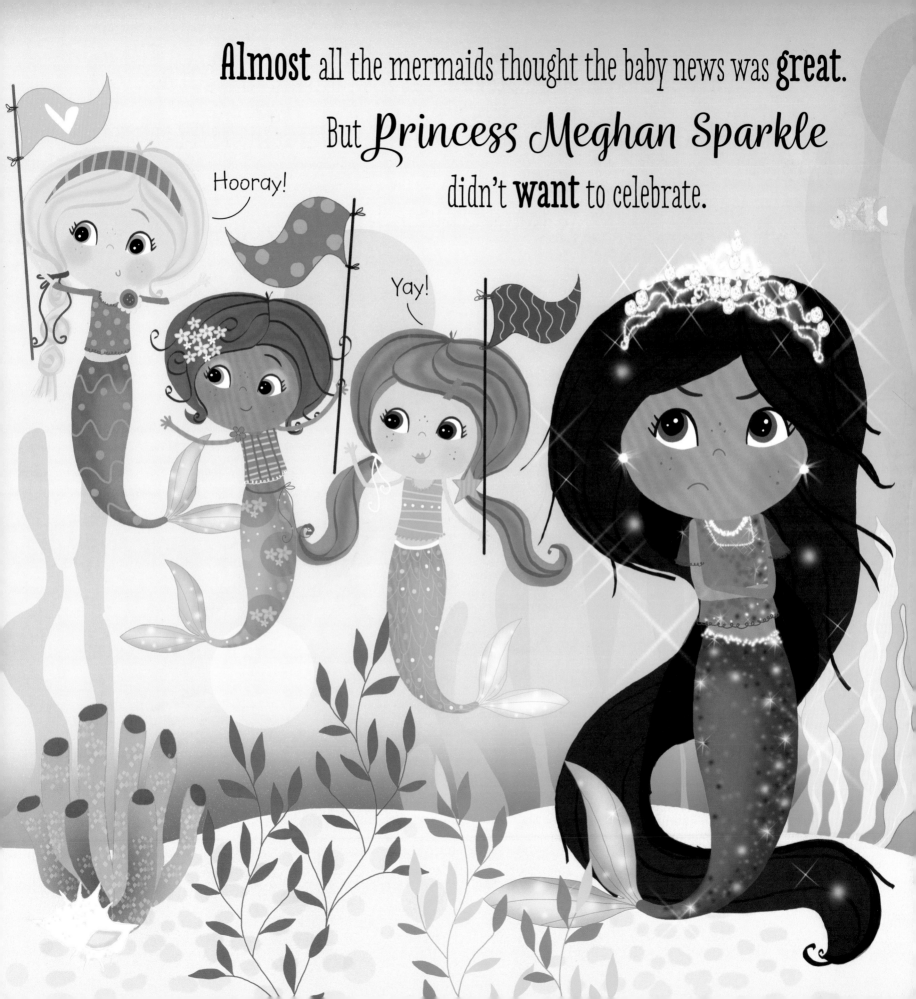

Almost all the mermaids thought the baby news was **great**.
But *Princess Meghan Sparkle* didn't **want** to celebrate.

Hooray!

Yay!

She was baby Bubble's **sister**, but she found it all a **bore**.
From *Meghan's* point of view, her life was going **fine** before!

She could **play games** in the castle or **sing loudly** if she chose...

La - la - LAA!

...and always found a **quiet** place
to **read** or have a **doze**.

But now, the baby **screamed** so much,
it drove her up the wall,
and **smelled** so bad that *Meghan*
couldn't concentrate at all!

Wahhhh

One day, Meghan couldn't wait to read her book somewhere, when suddenly the sound of Bubble's **crying** filled the air.

but every room was **smelly**...

Wahhhh!

Wahhhh!

Wahhhh!

So Meghan searched for somewhere **far away** from all the noise,

full...

or **stuffed** with baby toys!

She slammed her book closed with a SMACK and shouted,
"IT'S NOT FAIR!

Everyone's gone baby mad: I can't read ANYWHERE."

She sped outside and swam along
a winding path at speed,
until she found a silent spot:
the **PERFECT** place to read!

Wahhhhhhhhh!
wahhh!

Meghan read her book for **hours**,
as **happy** as a clam.

But **when** she tried to leave,
she cried...

"I don't know where I am!"

Clownfish Corner

She'd swum out here too **quickly**,
and forgotten to keep track.
So now she simply **didn't know**
which path would take her back!

Just when she felt **all at sea**,
the princess heard a cough.
The **mail-turtle** was swimming by,
dropping parcels off.

Seaweed Stables

Whale Way

"**Your Royal Highness!**" Turtle cried,
and gave a little bow.

"Can you help me?" **Meghan** asked.
"I've **lost my way** somehow!"

"I'll take you home," said Turtle, "but I **must** drop off this mail."
"**That sounds fun!**" the mermaid said, and joined him on his trail.

First, he had a parcel for the **clownfish** family,
who all lived **cramped together** in a small anemone.

"That looks **crowded**," Meghan thought,
and watched the clownfish play.
"I'm **lucky** I don't share a room
with Bubble every day."

Ooooh!

OoooooooOoh!

A choir **singing** whale songs
was the next stop on their rounds.

But **Meghan** couldn't **understand**
the group's **unusual** sounds.

Ooooooooh!

Ooooooooooh!

Turtle laughed:
"That's how they **speak**:
it just sounds odd to **you**."

Meghan thought of **Bubble's cries** ...
could they mean something too?

Meghan and the turtle
watched the babies for a while.

"Maybe siblings **are** ok,"
thought Meghan with a smile.

With the packages delivered,
Meghan thought of what she'd seen.
And **suddenly** she realised
how **silly** she had been!

She said, "I **understand** now
that when all is said and done,
having someone **new** around
is going to be **fun!**"

The turtle guided Meghan back across the ocean floor, and soon she heard a distant cry she **knew** she'd heard before.

Wahhhhhhhh!

"Thank you, Turtle!"
Meghan said.
"I recognise those sounds."
And then she followed Bubble's cries
into the castle grounds.

She rushed to **hug** the baby, feeling happy as can be.
"Hello Bubble," *Meghan* said. "I'm glad we're family."

After that, she didn't leave the royal baby's side, and read her **favourite** books aloud whenever Bubble cried.

Once upon a time...

So Meghan found some lovely friends, and as young Bubble grew,

she saw that life is wonderful when you are one of two!